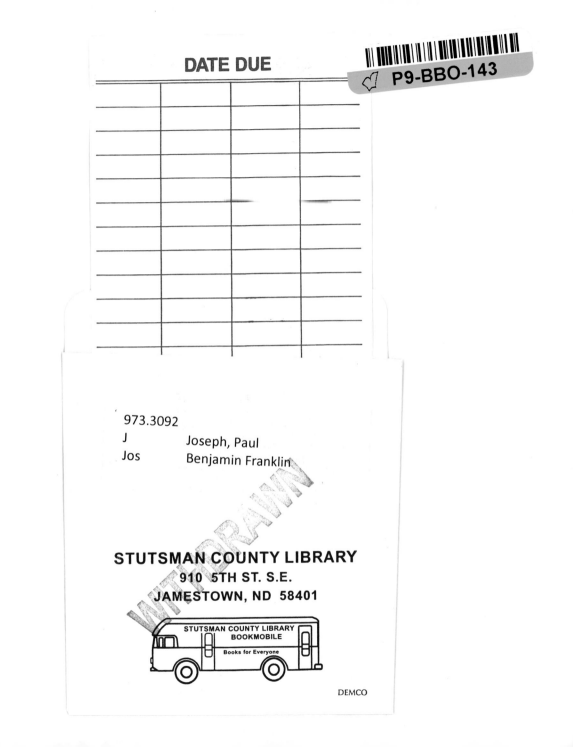

INVENTORS

BENJAMIN FRANKLIN

PAUL JOSEPH
ABDO & Daughters

Published by Abdo & Daughters, 4940 Viking Drive, Suite 622, Edina, Minnesota 55435.

Copyright © 1996 by Abdo Consulting Group, Inc., Pentagon Tower, P.O. Box 36036, Minneapolis, Minnesota 55435 USA. International copyrights reserved in all countries. No part of this book may be reproduced in any form without written permission from the publisher.

Printed in the United States.

Cover illustration and icon: Kristen Copham
Interior photos: Bettmann
Photo colorization: Professional Litho

Edited by Bob Italia

Library of Congress Cataloging-in-Publication Data

Joseph, Paul, 1970-
Benjamin Franklin / Paul Joseph.
  p. cm. — (Inventors)
Includes index.
Summary: Focuses on Franklin's creative ideas and inventions while also referring to his accomplishments as a writer, publisher, government official, and patriot.
  ISBN l-56239-633-1
l. Franklin, Benjamin, 1706-1790—Juvenile literature. 2. Inventors—United States—Biography—Juvenile literature. [1. Franklin, Benjamin, 1706-1790. 2. Inventors.]
I. Title. II. Series: Inventors (Series)
T40.F68J67   1996
973.3' 092--dc20
[B]   95-52414
                                                      CIP
                                                      AC

Contents

Early Years 4

Apprentice to His Brother 6

Reading and Writing 10

Benjamin Heads to Philadelphia 12

A Family, New Ideas,
   and Inventions 14

Glasses and the *Almanack* 16

His Best Invention 19

He Wore Many Hats 24

Glossary 28

Index 32

Early Years

When Benjamin Franklin was born on January 17, 1706, his father, Josiah, believed his son would be a very special person—maybe a **preacher**—and do great things. Benjamin was the 10th and last son. He was the youngest son of a youngest son of a youngest son of a youngest son of a youngest son—a pattern that lasted all the way back to his great-great grandfather!

In school, Benjamin was the head of his class. He loved learning, especially reading and **arithmetic**. He was also excellent in **Latin**. The teachers at his school knew that this young boy would go far.

Benjamin didn't do great deeds as a preacher. But he was special, and changed the course of history as an inventor, author, and **patriot**.

Portrait of Benjamin Franklin.

Apprentice to His Brother

When he was 10 years old, Benjamin began to help in his father's candle shop. There, he cut candlewicks and filled molds. By the time he was 12, Benjamin had finished school and was ready to work. His father wanted him to become an **apprentice**. An apprentice had to sign a paper pledging obedience and loyalty to a master until the age of 21 years.

Benjamin did not want to become an apprentice. Within two years, he would know all there was to know about the business—and still be stuck for seven years under a master. Instead, young Benjamin was already thinking of people's rights and **independence**.

Young Benjamin Franklin worked in his father's candle shop in Boston at the age of 10.

After much arguing, Josiah persuaded Benjamin to go into the printing business and be an **apprentice** under his brother, James.

Working for James was not fun. Benjamin did most of the work and got little pay. He knew that there were bigger things to accomplish. He couldn't stand the idea of working as an apprentice for another seven years.

Opposite page: Benjamin Franklin as an apprentice in the print shop of his brother, James.

Reading and Writing

In his spare time, Benjamin liked to write **poetry** and short stories. He also wrote newspaper articles and letters to the editor.

Benjamin used all his extra money to buy books. He was constantly reading. He read a book on **vegetarianism** and decided to quit eating meat. He read a book on swimming that described unusual tricks. He tried many of these tricks and even made-up some of his own. Benjamin would lie on his back in the water, hold a kite string, and let the kite pull him across the pond. It worked wonderfully, and people often watched in amazement.

Benjamin was always thinking of new ideas and inventions. He was very curious as a young man which continued throughout his life.

Young Benjamin Franklin selling his own ballads and poems in Boston.

Benjamin Heads to Philadelphia

Benjamin's main goal was to figure out how a person could make work easier, life more comfortable, and at the same time get ahead in the world. He knew that he could not reach that goal being an **apprentice** in Boston.

So at the age of 17, Benjamin ran away from his brother. He boarded a boat and ended up in Philadelphia, Pennsylvania.

Benjamin found a job with a **printer** and began earning his own money. He enjoyed his life in Philadelphia because of his new-found freedom.

Benjamin met many friends and even formed a club with other young men who liked to read, study, **debate**, and try new ideas. They would meet every Friday night and discuss many different subjects.

At age 22, Franklin started his own print shop in Philadelphia.

Things were going great for Benjamin. By the age of 22, he had his own print shop and newspaper, *The Pennsylvania Gazette.*

A Family, New Ideas, and Inventions

In 1730, Benjamin married Deborah Read. They had three children: Francis, Sarah, and William.

From 1730 to 1748, Benjamin worked hard in the printing business and became very successful. Because he was such a fine craftsman, Benjamin was made official printer for the **government** of Pennsylvania.

Although Benjamin was very busy, he still made time to try new ideas. He had many **theories** on why things happen. He wrote about **comets** and **hurricanes**.

Benjamin also had ideas to make his city better. He helped organize Philadelphia's first fire department. He devised the first circulating library in America. And he suggested ways to light the streets at night, dispose of garbage, and remove snow and ice from streets and sidewalks.

Many times, Benjamin created new inventions. He made a rocking chair with a fan over it. When he rocked, the fan would turn and keep the flies away. He made the first ladder with wheels so he could get books down from high shelves without getting off his ladder.

Benjamin also invented an iron stove.   This produced more heat than an ordinary fireplace, cost less to operate, was less smoky, and became very popular.

Glasses and the *Almanack*

Many of Benjamin's ideas were just for fun. But some made a huge impact on society. Two of his ideas are used more today than ever before.

One invention was bifocal eyeglasses. They helped people who needed two types of lenses to see and read. The top of the bifocal lense helped people see faraway. The bottom of the lense helped people see close-up, such as small type in books.

Another idea still popular today is *Poor Richard's Almanack*. Benjamin first published this book when he was 26. He thought people needed

Opposite page: Portrait of Benjamin Franklin wearing his invention, the bifocal glasses.

extra pieces of information and advice. It had maps, weather forecasts, schedule of tides, times for sunrises and sunsets, and a yearly calendar.

Benjamin put his own how-to hints in the *Almanack*, such as "A penny saved is a penny earned," and "Eat to live, not live to eat." Sometimes he added humorous one-liners, like: "Fish and visitors smell in three days."

Poor Richard's Almanack sold 10,000 copies a year, making it one of the bestselling books of its time. Benjamin continued to publish it for 25 years. Today, many publishers write their own almanacs.

His Best Invention

One of Benjamin's greatest **theories** was that **electricity** and lightning are the same.

Benjamin read much about electricity. He bought electrical equipment and learned how to perform tricks with electricity. Once, he got careless. Instead of shocking a turkey as he had planned, he took the whole shock through his own arms and body and was knocked to the ground.

Benjamin believed that electricity can come from lightning. At the time, most people were afraid of lightning and did not understand it.

Benjamin was determined to prove his electricity theory. He wrote to **scientists** and told them to put an iron rod on top of a high tower during a storm. Benjamin knew that electricity was attracted to iron rods.

Benjamin Franklin's

1706
Born Jan. 17th Boston, MA.

1716
Works in father's candle shop.

1718
Becomes an apprentice printer.

1723
Arrives in Philadelphia.

1728
Opens printing shop.

1753
Becomes deputy postmaster general for all colonies.

1757
Sent as representative to England.

1774
Becomes first postmaster general for all colonies.

1775
Helps draft Declaration of Independence.

1778
Helps draft Articles of Confederation.

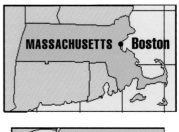

MASSACHUSETTS • Boston

Detail Area

PENNSYLVANIA

Philadelphia ✳

Life & Invention Timeline

1730
Marries Deborah Read.

1732
Publishes first *Poor Richard's Almanack.*

1737
Becomes deputy postmaster of Philadelphia.

1744
Invents Franklin stove.

1752
Conducts electricity experiment.

1781
Helps negotiate peace with England.

1784
Invents bifocals.

1787
Becomes President of Penn. Assembly and member of Constitutional Congress.

1790
Benjamin Franklin dies.

Three scientists in **Europe** tried the **experiment** and it worked. Benjamin was right: electricity and lightning were the same.

Benjamin wanted to do the lightning experiment himself, but Philadelphia did not have a tall tower. Instead, he made a kite with a long, pointed wire at the tip. Then he tied a key to the end of the kite string. On a stormy day, he flew the kite and felt the electric shock come through the key to his hand.

Benjamin became famous throughout America and the world. The King of France sent him congratulations. And English royalty presented him with a medal.

Opposite page: Franklin conducts an experiment to prove lightning is electricity.

He Wore Many Hats

Benjamin wanted to spend all his time working on inventions. But he knew there was more he could do for his country.

Benjamin became **Postmaster General**. He organized a new system so that it took only six days instead of six weeks for a letter to travel from Boston to Philadelphia.

Because Benjamin was so smart, the American **government** asked him to go to England and keep good relations with the English government. He worked there for 18 years until finally he had had enough. England was trying to take advantage of America with high **taxes**.

Benjamin came home in 1775 and worked with others to gain **independence** from England. He drafted and signed the Declaration of Independence, which gave America freedom from England.

Benjamin knew what it was like to be an **apprentice**. He didn't want himself or anyone from his country to live like one.

In 1776, the U.S. government sent Benjamin to France. He had to persuade the French to help America in its fight for independence. After a long struggle, Benjamin won the French over. On February 6, 1778, France signed the Treaty of Paris, pledging support for America. Benjamin was called the champion of liberty.

Benjamin remained in France as a representative until 1785. When he returned to Philadelphia, bells were rung and cannons were fired in his honor. For an entire week, the city celebrated his return.

Benjamin became president of the Pennsylvania Assembly, a post equal to that of governor. He was also a member of the Constitutional Convention, which wrote the **U.S. Constitution**.

Benjamin spent the last five years of his life in Philadelphia. He wrote more newspaper articles and his famous autobiography. He died at the age of 84 on April 17, 1790.

Benjamin Franklin will be remembered as a man who wore many hats. He was a writer, an inventor, a publisher, a **government** official, and a **patriot**. But most of all, he was a person who cared about freedom—freedom for everyone.

Opposite page: Benjamin Franklin crowned his accomplishments as a diplomat and fighter for freedom by serving as a member of the Constitutional Convention of 1787.

Glossary

apprentice (uh-PREN-tiss) - A person who signs a paper saying he or she will work for a master until the age of 21. During this time, the apprentice learns about the business.

arithmetic (uh-RITH-muh-tick) - The type of math that deals with adding, subtracting, multiplying, and dividing numbers.

comet - A heavenly body made up of ice and dust that looks like a star with a cloudy tail of light.

debate (dee-BAIT) - To discuss or sometimes argue a question or topic.

electricity (e-lek-TRISS-uh-tee) - A current or power.

Europe - Many countries across the Atlantic Ocean which make up this continent. It is the second smallest continent next to Australia.

experiment (ek-SPARE-uh-ment) - The process of testing in order to discover.

government (GUV-er-ment) - The group that runs and makes laws for either the country, state, district or city.

hurricane (HER-uh-kane) - A large, tropical storm with violent wind and very heavy rain.

independence (in-dee-PEN-dense) - A freedom from the control, influence, or help of others.

Latin - A language of the ancient Romans that children use to study in school.

patriot (PAY-tree-it) - A person who loves his or her country and gives it loyal support.

poetry (POH-uh-tree) - A style of writing that is often arranged in patterns of lines, rhymes, and rhythms.

Postmaster General - The head of the entire post-office in the country.

preacher - A person who advises and speaks on religious subjects. A minister.

printer - A person whose business or work is printing on paper, such as newspapers, books, magazines, etc.

scientist (SIGH-un-tist) - Someone very smart in science who studies and investigates questions, and comes up with answers.

sermon (SIR-mun) - A speech given by a preacher in front of the congregation.

taxes - Money paid by people to support the government.

theory - An explanation of something based on observation.

U.S. Constitution - The written set of principles by which the United States is governed.

vegetarianism - The act of never eating food that comes from an animal.

Index

A

apprentice 6, 8, 12, 25
autobiography 26

B

Boston (MA) 12, 24
brother 8
business 6, 8

C

calendar 18
circulating library 15
comets 14
Constitutional Convention 26
country 25

D

death 26
Declaration of Independence 25

E

electricity 19, 22
England 24
English royalty 22
Europe 22

F

father 4, 6
fire department 15
France 25
Franklin, Francis 14
Franklin, James 8

Franklin, Josiah 4, 8
Franklin, Sarah 14
Franklin, William 14

G

great-great grandfather 4

H

how-to hints 18
hurricanes 14

I

ideas 10, 14
independence 6, 24, 25
inventions 10, 15
inventor 4, 26
iron stove 15

K

King of France 22
kite 10, 22

L

ladder 15
light 15, 19, 22
lightning 19, 22

N

newspaper 13
newspaper articles 10, 26

P

patriot 4, 26
Pennsylvania 14
Pennsylvania Assembly 26
Pennsylvania Gazette 13
Philadelphia (PA) 12, 15, 22, 24, 25, 26
Poor Richard's Almanack 16, 18
Postmaster General 24
printing 12, 14
print shop 13
publisher 18, 26

R

Read, Deborah 14
rocking chair 15

S

school 4, 6

T

taxes 24
theories 14, 19
Treaty of Paris 25

U

U.S. Constitution 26

V

vegetarianism 10